One Stormy Night

Story by Joy Cowley
Illustrations by Kathleen O'Malley

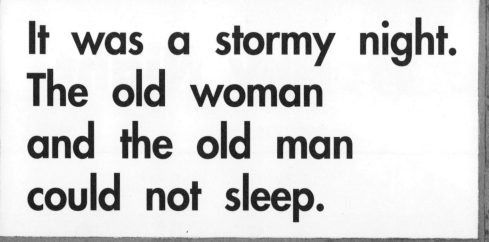

It was a stormy night.
The old woman
and the old man
could not sleep.

2

Out in their street
the wind went
Whooo! Whooo! Whoo!

Out by their mailbox
the owl went
Hooo! Hooo! Hoo!

Out in their yard
the trees went
Swish! Swish! Swish!

Out by their steps
the rain went
Splish! Splish! Splish!

Out on their roof
the shingles went
Flappity, flap!

Out on their porch
the shutters went
Tappity, tap!

Then,
the front door went
Creak! Creak! Creak!

Then,
the stairs went
Squeak! Squeak! Squeak!

The old man
and the old woman
sat up in bed.
"What is that?" they cried.

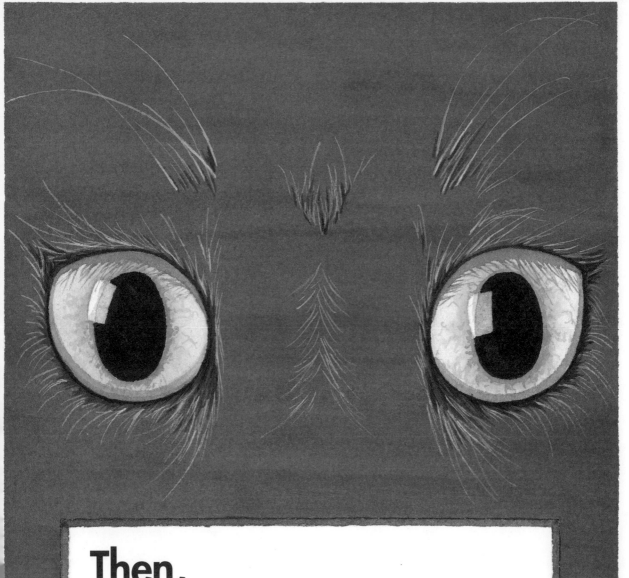

Then,
something jumped
on their bed and went
YOWL!

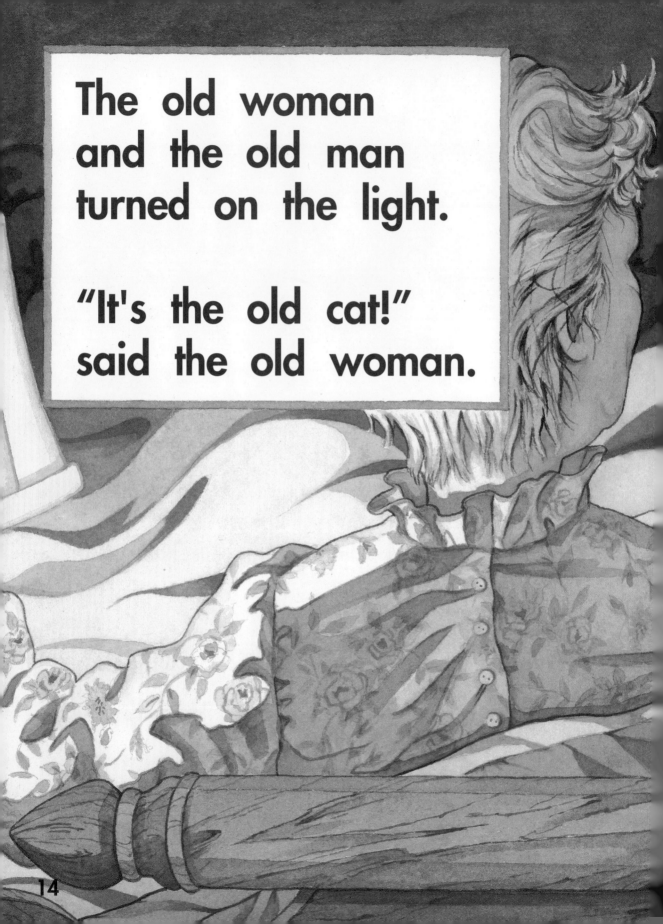

The old woman
and the old man
turned on the light.

"It's the old cat!"
said the old woman.

"She's cold and wet!"
said the old man.

Then the old man
and the old woman
and the old cat
curled up in the bed
and went to sleep.
Z-z-z-z! Z-z-z-z! Z-z-z-z!